The Things Nighttime Brings

Jamie Hitt

MW00887486

3 Bears Press

Published by 3 Bears Press 2021

Copyright © 2022 by Jamie Hitt

This book is a work of fiction. The characters, incidents, and dialogues are products of the author's imagination and are not to be construed as real. Any resemblance to actual persons, living or dead, is entirely coincidental.

All rights reserved. This book, or any portion thereof, may not be reproduced or used in any manner whatsoever, without the express written permission of the author, except for the use of brief quotations in a book review.

ISBN 978-1-7377566-4-4

To Jacob, Noah, and Syd.
May you always find beauty,
even in darkness.

Little Thomas the toad
crossed the old unpaved road
with a hip and a hop,
and a plippity-plop.

He jumped up and he slid
down a steep hill and hid,
and he said not a word
as he waited for Bird.

"She will not find me here,"
thought young Thomas with cheer.

but the branches then stirred,
and above him he heard
the soft sound of a tweet
that was lovely and sweet,
and he looked up to see
his friend laughing with glee.

Bird tagged him and flew -
that was Thomas's cue,
and he'd seek to the end
'til he found his new friend.

He looked low and then high –
Something red caught his eye –
he peered closer to see
and found Bird in a tree.

They continued to play
for the rest of the day,
and they had so much fun
they did not see the sun

Slowly fading away,
as the night replaced day.
But as the moon brightened,
Thomas soon became frightened.

He felt Scared deep within
because he'd never been
So far from his home,
So late, So alone.

Frightening Shadows appeared,
that grew large as he neared,
jumping right out at him
from behind each tree limb.

He could hear a Strange Sound,
as it floated around,
in the dark balmy air,
but he couldn't tell where,

and he couldn't even see,
as he hopped on blindly,
through the blackened meadow,
not knowing where to go.

Then he heard a "Tweet-tweet."
Oh, it sounded so sweet –
the most beautiful word
from his good friend the bird.

She had found him again,
and she flashed him a grin,
as though she wasn't scared
and she had not a care.

She landed near him,
when She Saw he looked grim,
and She tweeted a Song
that helped make him feel Strong.

Thomas started to hop,
and he tried not to stop,
as Bird led them along
while still singing her song.

Once again came that sound,
and he looked all around
in each flower and tree
to see what it could be.

Then Bird pointed up high,
to a branch in the sky,
where a tawny owl stood
hooting loud as he could.

"Croak croak," Thomas said,
as the owl bowed his head,
giving him a kind smile -
Still hooting all the while.

Croak

Croak

Thomas felt slightly stronger,
as he hopped a bit longer
with a little less fear
of that sound in his ear.

Then Bird pointed ahead,
with her wings widely spread,
to a beautiful sight
full of dancing moonlight –

that glittered and gleamed
on the water that seemed
to shine brightly like jewels
in small radiant pools.

Thomas felt so amazed,
as he and Bird gazed
at the moon and the stars,
that twinkled up so far,

as they filled up the night
with their soft glowing light,
and he felt less afraid
there and then in that glade.

Then to his surprise,
something bright caught his eyes,
as a star shot up high
'cross the darkened night sky,
leaving there in its trail
a soft shimmering tail,
and he thought that it might
be his favorite sight.

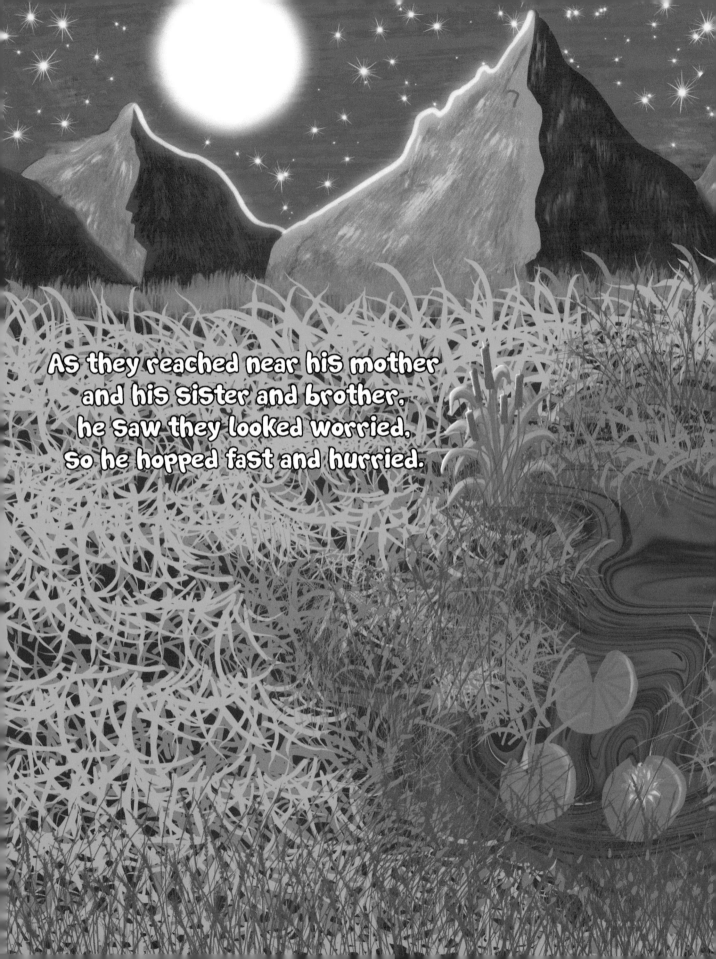

As they reached near his mother
and his sister and brother,
he saw they looked worried,
so he hopped fast and hurried.

He soon told them all
of what he could recall
of his fear of the night
and his love of moonlight.

And as Bird flew away
Thomas thought of their day –
he felt braver somehow,
and he realized now,
he was no longer scared
and was glad Bird had shared

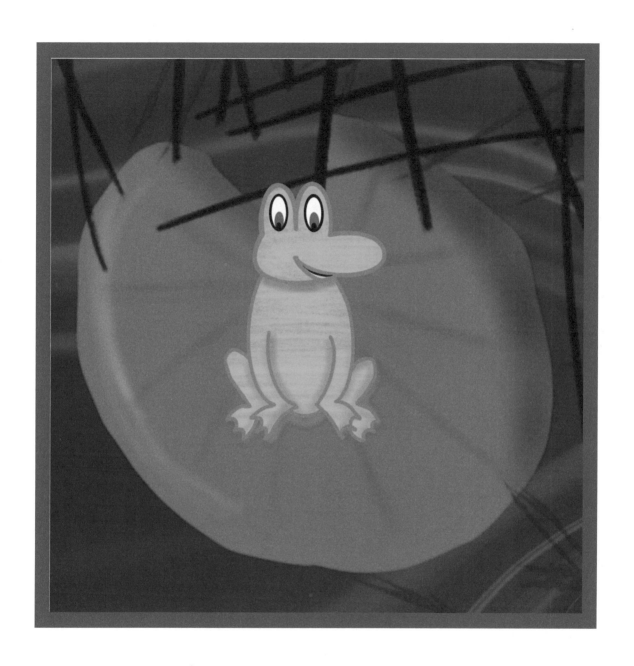

all the wonderful things
that nighttime brings.

ABOUT THE AUTHOR

Jamie Hitt has always been enchanted by the magic and wonder of children's books, and she started writing stories at a young age. After working for 10 years in the corporate world, she decided to go back to school to pursue her true passions. She obtained a Master's Degree in Humanities, with an emphasis in Creative Writing, and found her way to writing children's stories once again. When she's not writing and drawing, you can find her spending time with her husband and three young children at their home in Southern California.

READ MORE THOMAS THE TOAD

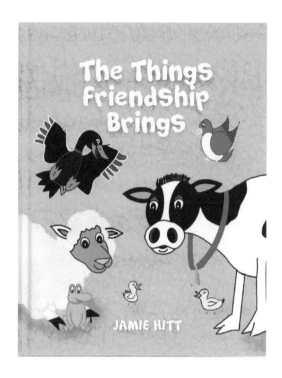

"Tweet tweet," says a bird to young Thomas the Toad as he is out for an afternoon hop. Thomas is drawn to the beautiful language that the bird speaks, but he doesn't understand it. Nor does he understand the words he hears from the duck, the cow, or the sheep. Thomas longs to make friends with these other animals, but he doesn't know how to make friends when they don't speak the same language. Thomas must learn to embrace the differences of the other animals around him, and find new ways to say the things friendship brings.

CPSIA information can be obtained
at www.ICGtesting.com
Printed in the USA
LVHW070328290322
714678LV00002B/33

* 9 7 8 1 7 3 7 7 5 6 6 4 4 *